GULF OF GUINEA

A true collection of original short stories: Open your eyes to life in West Africa! Like the many rivers that drain into the GULF OF GUINEA; these stories will spark your curiosity in the West African culture and its many characters whose innocent, unfiltered and organic, spirited dialogue will arouse your senses and give you insight and appreciation of this rich and fragrant land and its people.

From online reviews:
A taste of Africa in delightful short stories:
Definitely a good read. From the start, you are drawn into this exotic world, with its unique and colorful characters – and somehow you have the impression you have met them, or someone like them. The settings introduce you to the West African lifestyle – in your mind, you can almost hear the music in the background, or hear their accent, or smell the spicy mouth-watering foods. I learned quite a lot about this region, while having a good time.

I wish the author develops some of these rich short stories into a novel – I for one would be sure to buy it!
By Amazon Customer

These short stories are great, fun and a quick read! Left me wanting to hear more from these colorful characters, especially the crazy women! I had a good laugh and learned a few things too about another culture.
By another Amazon Customer

GULF OF GUINEA

GEORGE NII AMON ASHIE

Gulf of Guinea, a collection of short stories

George Nii Amon Ashie

Publisher's Note: This is a work of fiction. Names, characters, places, and incidents are a product of the author's imagination. Locales and public names are sometimes used for atmospheric purposes. Any resemblance to actual people, living or dead, or to businesses, companies, events, institutions, or locales is completely coincidental.

Book Layout ©2013 BookDesignTemplates.com

Gulf of Guinea / George Nii Amon Ashie. -- 1st ed.

ISBN 978-0-9969976-0-7

Contents

UFOs DON'T SWING BY FOR EXERCISE

DANCE TO THE BONE

PRODUCTS OF PASSION

ONE WAY TICKET TO KANO

GULF OF GUINEA

NOTES

ACKNOWLEDGMENTS

Thank you to the treasures of my heart who encouraged me to never give up until this book was completed, edited and published. Thank you so much for urging me on in spite of my own numerous doubts and self-inflicted setbacks!

ONE

UFOS DON'T SWING BY

FOR EXERCISE

I remember one maid we had when I was growing up. She tried very hard to please my Mama, who made it her business to make any maid look incompetent. It did not bother us much because we kids knew Mama, and we knew that's what she did sometimes to get her kicks. However, the last six maids did not see things the same way. They packed up and took off. It usually happened shortly after Dad did something to tick Mama off. Then for the poor maid, it was sheer misery 24-hours-a-day! We had almost given up on anyone staying, when Ama showed up one morning, fresh from the country.

A distant relative had brought her to our house at Mama's request to teach her "niece" some proper etiquette. It was more like Russian roulette African style with six sharp ten-foot spears and no shields.

Mama was in a hurry. She had changed her traditional cloth outfit twice already. The Ga-Mashie Women's Social Club meeting started at 5 o'clock. It was already 6 o'clock and the maid had not yet returned with the slip she wanted pressed.

"If I lay my hands on that twit I will cut off her left nostril and fry it in her thick greasy nose!" Mama said to herself in a slow rumble. Between you and me, the slip was late because Ama was already a bag of nerves from three tongue lashings she had received earlier in the afternoon. Every day was identical, well almost, with a few variations like... which day of the week it was!

Ama got up early, she would hurry to prepare Mama's bath and then get the twins ready for school. She either got cussed out for not taking a bath herself first and thus, "Insulting the air of my bedroom with your 3-week-old sweat!" or when she did take a bath, she still got cussed for wasting water by taking too long in the makeshift shower behind the servants' quarters. Yes, Mama had eyes that never slept, although she snored like something between a broken Morse code machine and the national anthem.

"Here's your slip Ma'am." Ama said gracefully with down cast eyes, arms extended, displaying the pressed slip.

"Give me that thing and get out before I scrape the skin off your ugly back! Look! Now I am almost an hour late! What do you think the other Misses will think of me! Eh? The meeting will be over before I get there. Go tell that sloth of a driver to bring the car around before I get him fired!" Mama spat out without taking one breath!

Ama backed out of the bedroom, almost falling over the dozen or so discarded outfits Mama had tried on earlier.

"Stop dancing and get lost!" Mama added with venom. Ama flew down the stairs.

"Why did I have to be so lucky to always pick the clumsiest maids?" Mama asked herself chuckling. "Lord help me! I better get dressed. Klotey should have the car ready by now."

Mama sprayed herself with half a bottle of her husband's favorite eau-du-cologne. She walked out briskly to the front of the house and fired off rapid orders to us before placing her large bottom squarely in the middle of the back seat of the old Valiant.

"Don't forget to cook the roast slowly Ama, and wash the twins properly before you put them in the bed!... and you! ... (that was me) you better clean your room before I get back! Big Sister, see to it that the Darkos bring my niece over to visit on Sunday. I'll be back by eight. "Klotey let's go!" Sure Mom, we'll all be in bed by the time you get back at ten o'clock, unless of course, Dad keeps us up with those wild ghost stories of his youth. Maybe I'll tell you more about that later.

"What do they do at all those meetings she goes to, Big Sister?" I asked looking up at her squinting.

"I wouldn't worry about that if I was you Poogie. Just go and clean your room before she finds something awful to do to you when she gets back!" I disappeared into the dusk.

Every now and then I wondered why the twins were called twins. They did not look or act anything like each other or for that matter, like anyone of us. My oldest brother had a theory.

"A pair of identical space ships fell out from the sky and dropped them on us." He'd say and laugh by himself. Big Bro, whom we sometimes called AB, short for Alien

Brother, was into two types of UFOs; Unidentified Flying Objects and Uninterrupted Female Ogling. "One day, one of these girls is going to grab your balls and run!" Mama used to warn him.

The twins however, apparently considered themselves a real pair. They never tired of playing this trick on Ama. One of them would get in the bathtub while the other sat on the toilet seat and watched. Whenever Ama turned away to grab the soap or a towel, they'll switch places. They would do this over and over again, until she lost track of whose hair was washed last or who was ready to be rinsed off. Finally, out of sheer frustration, she would explode. Grab them by the ears, yank them out of the bathroom, rinsed off or not and dump them on the bed! Then ignoring cries of "Witch! Evil witch!" and "We're gonna tell Mommy!!", she would rub them down vigorously with the first piece of dry cloth in sight, tuck them under a faded Mickey Mouse bed sheet and storm out of their bedroom forgetting to turn off the light. Yep, and Mama always got her for that one. I will tell you one thing though; this 5 ft. 1 in. maid had spirit. She never gave up.

One day, her perseverance paid off big time. Two of

us, were happy for her. Guess. Homowo is a big festival celebrated in August to thank ancestors, gods and goddesses for a good harvest. Twins, acknowledged as a symbol of abundance, a gift from some benign deity, play a big role in the festivities. During the big parade, usually the high point of the celebrations, a few party-hearty deities or spirits have been known to exercise visitation rights on a number of taciturn twins, and a few innocent bystanders too!

The hosts thus accosted, usually ended up performing poly-symphonic contortions of infinite rhythms and alacrity, the envy of any self-proclaimed yogi from the Himalayas! This year, our twins wanted to participate in the parade. Big Brother AB said they must have been trained by Martian dancers. The unsuspecting spirits that possessed them had a hard time keeping up with the little firecrackers!

The crowd will rush back to get away from one of them, only to find the other right behind with a sinister smile waiting for them! There was a noxious familiar smell in the air. I'd never seen so many people shit in their Sunday clothes before.

Ama, on the other hand, was having the time of her life. Three husky guys from the Bukom Tough Guys

Club were chatting her up. She wore a beautiful red dress Big Sister had made for her. The combination of the dress, the large band of colorful beads around her neck and the red hibiscus flower she wore in her hair brought out a side of her we had never seen before. Then when Alien Brother removed his shades to take another look, I knew she was in trouble. UFO's don't swing by for exercise! Ah yes, the red dress.

Big Sister had promised Ama the dress by the day of the parade if she could just hang in there with Mama's quirks and kamikaze diatribe. Well, Ama dug in her heels and beat the odds. Big Sister, who was a much sought-after seamstress, made her an exquisite dress. Looking at Ama that morning just before we left for the parade, I knew she must have poured herself into that red dress. No gaps, loose ends, threads, or seams were to be found anywhere between her and the dress! So, on that hot August afternoon, she stole the thunder from the twins' feats of magic!

The Honorable James Nkansah Thompson, Minister of Trade and All Celebrations, showed up in his imported Mercedes-Benz 220D and whisked Ama away from us forever. When Mama found out, she called him a few names I would rather not print here. Use your elastic imagination. Then when she was done with him, the local government, the state government, the organizers of the festival, the gods and goddesses in attendance were all served an equally potent dish of Mama's own kind of verbal venom.

It took three days of self-induced "that ungrateful, no-good, horny wretch of a bitch" incantations before she calmed down.

Well, and as usual AB had the last word: "Mama come down to earth, she's gone! Nkansah Thompson's eyes must be big as flying saucers!" AB muttered under his breath dismayed, "How did he pick her out of all those fine babes at the parade?"

TWO

DANCE TO THE BONE

The colorful red, gold and green banner read in bold black letters:

TONIGHT, AT TIP TOE NIGHT CLUB,
THE BEST INDEPENDENCE DAY
DANCE!
`DANCE TO THE BONE'
KWESI GYAMFI AND THE HIGHLIFE
MASTERS WILL SHAKE YOU WITH SU-
PER AFROBEAT AND HIGHLIFE HITS!
SEE YOU THERE!

Excitement was already building in the city. Super star trumpet player, Kwesi Gyamfi and his Highlife Masters had been away on tour in the northern region and Upper Volta for more than three months. This was going to be their first gig in the city, the band's base of operation.

Jemima was putting finishing touches to her new dress for the dance tonight. Music from `Dance To The Bone', the Highlife Masters' international smash hit song, filled every room in her house with sharp horn section blasts and ethnic percussion riffs from the £100,000 stereo her last lover from Nigeria bought for her in Lagos for Christmas last year. Christmas presents were not taken lightly in Lagos. Merely breaking up with your lover over a cheap present was neither acceptable nor enough. You were a lucky man if all you lost was the lady. In fact, it was downright dangerous to be stingy. Horror stories about what happened to these tight-elbowed men usually surfaced around the beginning of January, after, as the female editor of one local tabloid puts it, "The men had been given sufficient time to do the honorable thing". Jemima must have had a man who did her right. She loved her stereo and had all the latest hits in her record library. Everyone liked her parties because the music sounded so good playing on that awesome machine.

Tonight was special. She could feel it. Ted Quarshie was going to be at Tip Toe. "Some men just had it", she said aloud to herself, "Something that made a woman throw out all her pots and pans, before he even asks you out to a restaurant! No, I won't think too much about him walking over to ask me to dance. That would spoil the subtle look of innocent surprise I have been practicing in front of the mirror for the last two days!"

"One more time!" Screamed the assistant band leader and sometime music director, Mister Sonny Benson, as he insisted on being called. Mister Benson had a bachelor's degree in music from UNILAG, when he lived with an uncle in Ikeja, Lagos. Before that, he had already played with the best and greatest, from King Emmanuel Obe to Fela Ransom Kuti in Nigeria and E. T. Mensah's band and Jerry Hansen's Ramblers Dance band in Ghana. Twenty-two-year-old guitarist, Mac Pope was tired of the song. He had played it almost every night for the last year.

"This is exactly what I hate about hit songs", Mac

muttered under his breath, "The people, I mean the fans, never get tired of hearing the same damn tune for the umpteenth time!"

What most of the guys in the band did while zooming through the bars of a song, was check out the action on the dance floor. Most of the ladies moved well, wiggling and shaking with serious fun. Those that were not so fluid were otherwise engaged, grasping some long-belly sugar daddy sweating profusely in a tight suit. Sometimes it was very funny. The cats would look at one another and burst out laughing in the middle of one of Kwesi Gyamfi's trumpet solos. Kwesi was cool. He knew what was happening. He would just grin between breaths and blow on.

Mac remembered the ladies of the North, and a gentle smile appeared on his face. "Falina," he whispered her name and sighed. She would be coming to Accra next week. She told him their last night together in Bolgatanga. It was a good thing Adjele got tired of their on-again-off-again love affair and left... but he missed her.

"Mac play dat solo! Why, you young man, how come you have so much to think about and you haven't even fathered a child yet?" Mister Benson yelled and the whole band roared with laughter. Mac's fingers burned the guitar strings, complex melodies and harmonies screamed out of his amp, and everyone shut up. "This boy is great", Mister Benson thought to himself and sighed.

"As a matter of fact, he is very good." Sonny Benson knew that most of the band's young fans came to their shows because of Mac's virtuosity on the instrument. Especially those wild guitar solos he played like, what's his name? Ginny Kendrix? No, Papa, "Jimi Hendrix!!!!" his teenage daughter always corrected him. "Hey, when I read music at Ikeja, that boy was probably crawling around in diapers!" Mister Benson would reply.

"Okay, boys, see you all tonight, eight o'clock sharp at Tip Toe. Don't be late!" Mister Benson yelled, as he put away his sheet music and horn, and then walked out the room briskly.

It was six o'clock. This was the third time in a row it had happened. The clasp on the back of Jemima's dress kept breaking each time she tried to wiggle into the dress. She was getting frustrated. "Urrr! Why did I eat so much this late?" She had been so busy she forgot to eat an early lunch. Now she may not fit into the dress. The dress was intentionally cut to tight specifications to enhance every curve on her full body. The seamstress did her job. Then she did hers, eat like a fool! What was she going to do? Her girlfriend, Lizzy, would be arriving any minute now. They had to get to Tip Toe early to get a good seat close to the dance floor and the bandstand. "Stupid! Stupid! Stupid!" Jemima screamed stomping her foot in rhythm to the Afrobeat song blaring from the speakers. "Boy, is it hot!" She was sweating. "That light soup had too much pepper in it." Her bowels growled. She quickly peeled off the half-worn dress and hurried to the toilet.

"Knock, knock, anybody home?" Lizzy yelled through the open front door.

"Shit! Can't anyone take a shit in peace?" Jemima hissed under her breath. "I'm in the bathroom, but don't come in here." She yelled between grunts, "Your perception of me may be permanently damaged!" Lizzy walked into the house cautiously. She headed for the bathroom door.

"Girl, what are you doing in there? We are going to be late!" Lizzy said alarmed.

"I ate too much. Now my new dress won't fit." Jemima said groaning. Lizzy burst out laughing and said,

"Good for Ted, he wouldn't have to rip it off!"

Jemima started to laugh and stopped immediately in

the middle of a convulsion. "Shut up, please. I can't laugh and do this." She pleaded with her friend.

"I know it's serious business", Lizzy retorted, "but.." and they both burst out laughing again.

"Stop Lizzy, or I'll come out right now!" said Jemima.

"Oh, please don't do that." Lizzy begged, chuckling. "What did you eat so much off anyway?"

"Don't even ask." Jemima replied. "I'm almost done." Five minutes later Jemima came out of the bathroom fully dressed. Lizzy whistled. "Ted Quarshie is in trouble tonight!" They both picked up the chorus of the song still playing on the stereo: "Dance, dance, dance, dance... dance to the bone! Oh yeah! Dance to the bone!"

THREE

PRODUCTS OF PASSION

Lantey avoided Tawiah when he was six. She was seven then. She would always tease him about being older than him. Age is reverenced in the clan. One always respected one's elders. It was a privilege the young ones looked forward to with enthusiasm. The elders, most of them, had earned this respect from selfless service to their families and communities. Tawiah was feisty. Her aunt teased her mother often about the searing passion that must have burned a crater right through the mattress the night Tawiah was conceived!

Tawiah's Dad was a sometime businessman, inventor, salesman, highlife band lead vocalist, sailor, political campaign manager, professional soccer player, the list was endless. His friends affectionately called him Chief Jack, i.e., jack-of-all-trades. Oh! I almost forgot his most cherished expertise, ladies' man. Jack was the epitome of sub-Sahara cool. In his own words, "I make the ladies feel at home, and mine, is where the action is." He never left home without his sunglasses, packet of cigarettes and auto-opening umbrella, dubbed 007.

Tawiah's mother, Serwah, had an equally impressive history, well in a different dimension so to speak. When she was finishing secondary school, she hung out with "international" businessmen. They would get her anything she wanted, all she had to do was lift her eyelids. Serwah was a sweet, vibrant and voluptuous young girl. She was well liked by everybody. She received invitations to all the house parties. When she showed up at your party, then you suddenly became vogue. This tradition continued well through her teens and into her early twenties. By then she was very much in demand, attending every major Presidential ball and dance held in the capital city. She was a beautiful young woman. Sometimes, her parents worried about her. "She'll never get married at this rate." Her mother would sigh. Reverend Odamtey, her favorite uncle, always came to her rescue.

"Leave her alone. She is still young. Let her enjoy the

gifts God has given her."

"Amen." Serwah will whisper to herself.

It was at the OAU Ball for visiting dignitaries from several African countries that a virtually unimportant braggart convinced her that maybe other men, outside her circle of international businessmen, could be exciting. The braggart was Jack Ashong, Chief Jack himself, lead singer of the All Stars Highlife Band. The Chief had half the ladies at the ball cracking up all night with his boyish antics and mixture of corny and dark humor jokes. Serwah liked him instantly.

Jack had to keep the guests entertained between sets, because the band leader who was usually the MC for their shows had a touch of laryngitis and was saving his wind for the serious bebop trumpet solos he blew. Thus, that night Jack added another skill to his long list of credentials, stand-up comic á la MC. His debut was even more memorable, because these ladies had the time of their lives laughing so much that the tears running down their faces ruined their makeup. A number of the more feisty ones almost beat him up when the band took a break, halfway through the ball. Serwah couldn't care less. She had her businessman by his short round legs.

She burst out laughing the loudest whenever Ashong told a good one. Jack noticed her right away, and sought her out whenever he got to the punch lines. Thus, began the first of many "unplanned" meetings. Serwah asked her international businessmen to take her out to every one of the band's shows, and on these occasions, she never spoke more than a few words to Jack. One day, Jack decided enough was enough. He was going to take the saucepan to the forest and bypass catching the game first. During the afternoon before the show, Jack added some fresh spice to his cache of smooth lines before the old mirror on the door of his wardrobe, polishing his rhetoric and carefully choreographed moves. Chief Jack must have done something right, because that night, Serwah laugh-ed louder than ever at his antics. Then later that evening, when Jack stopped by her table during one of the band's breaks, she took one look at him and burst out laughing all over again. In the midst of tear-gushing mirth she innocently accepted a date to "take in some beer" at the Labadi Beach Coconut Grove after work on Friday. Jack acknowledged her with his extra wide thirty-two-teeth smile, and Serwah just about suffocated herself with something between a snort, a squeal and booming laugh-ter from three diametrically opposite places somewhere within her body. Jack looked at her concerned.

"Oh shit! I hope I didn't kill you." Said Jack alarmed.

"Shut up or you just might. I want to live to tell my grandchildren about you, Mr. Ashong. You are worse than an ass." Serwah said gasping .

"How? Too big, too flabby or too stupid?" Jack asked grinning.

"All three." Serwah replied giggling and picked up her beer. Her businessman date laughed boisterously.

"Uh?" Jack piped up, twisting his neck and half the features on his face to look at his rear-end. Serwah dumped a sip of beer right back into her glass laughing.

"Go, go away, now! You are a crazy man." Serwah said laughing. Then she turned to her date, "I think we better go Mr. Asiedu before this man kills me with laughter. My sides hurt." she added with a pout.

"Alright, Mr. Ashong, good music. Thank you, thank you." Mr. Asiedu said and shook Jack's hand, leaving a 100 US dollar bill behind in his palm. Jack acknowledged him with a nod and said good night to Serwah.

Labadi Beach was only the beginning. At first she would spend a casual evening with Jack here and there. Soon, it became every two or three days. Then, Serwah suddenly woke up in bed with him one Saturday and realized that she had just spent three days with this man who was very different from the kind of man she liked to be seen with. He had given her nothing she could hold, hang around her neck, slip into her purse, or wear to show off at the next state dinner she attended. Serwah suddenly sat up straight in bed.

"What is happening to me? Am I losing my mind?" She asked herself alarmed. Then, she turned around and looked at the sleeping man beside her and smiled. "I want him." Serwah said softly to herself.

"Jack, Jack, wake up. Wake up! We'll be late for the wedding." Serwah raised her voice excitedly. Jack shot out of deep sleep in mid snore.

"Wedding? Did you say wedding? My baby sister just got married. Another husband?" Jack asked, opening his mouth to yawn. He never finished yawning. "Wait. Wait a minute. Who is getting married?" He asked. Serwah just sat there with an impish grin on her face. "Oh, no. No, you don't. No way, Serwah. What about Mr. Asiedu? Your international businessman, remember?" Jack pleaded. Serwah just shook her head.

"Jack, he is boring. All he does is buy me stuff. Besides he's an old man. You are young and strong and you

make me laugh." She replied patting his rear end lovingly.

"...But you'll live better with him. Life is no joking
matter. It involves yams, bread, butter, babies and office
work! ...And, er... I, I don't know about th... th... the last
two." Jack stammered.

"You'll learn," Serwah said, "... fast. Come on, we'll be
late. I don't want us to keep the Reverend waiting."

"You already called him? Aieeeeee! Woman!" Jack bu-
ried his face in the covers. "Who else knows about this?"

"Don't worry, no one. Just you and I and the Reverend," Serwah knew her man, "Oh, and I invited the
band, just kidding" she added, laughing at the look on his
face.

Jack went through that whole day in a daze. The Reverend Odamtey married them at the local church down
the street. He was glad his niece had finally decided to
settle down with a nice young man closer to her age. The
good Reverend chuckled to himself after congratulating
them, "Poor chap, doesn't know what has hit him yet."
Reverend Odamtey whispered to himself.

"Did you say something uncle?" Serwah asked him
and winked. The Reverend burst out in a vibrant boister-

ous laugh, the trademark of the family. He shook his head and walked out of the vestry.

Serwah took Jack's hand and led him out into the sunshine, all smiles.

"Where is the band?" She asked her new husband.

"What band, you didn't?" Jack asked back confused.

"Come on, Jack, we have to celebrate. This is our wedding day. I'd like to drink some champagne and slow dance with my new husband. Besides, I want the best for my wedding day, and you and the All Stars are. Yes, you are the best." Serwah said with a dazzling smile. Jack looked really befuddled. He searched his pockets frantically for a cigarette. Serwah opened her purse, took one out, kissed him first, then stuck the cigarette between his lips and lit it for him with a smile.

"Thanks. Now I need a drink." Jack said after a deep drag.

"A big one." Serwah added with a laugh. "You're going to need it before I'm through with you tonight." Jack looked at her sideways.

"Cheer up, my dear. I only married you because I love you very much. I want you to be happy. Those business-men never meant anything to me. I want to be with someone I love before I have my first child." Serwah was on a roll.

"God Almighty, Angel Gabriel, Abraham, Moses, somebody holy help me! Woman are you pregnant?" Jack asked cigarette butt flying out of his mouth.

"Not yet." replied Serwah with a smile. "But, who knows...", she added, "maybe I will be in a few hours." Jack bolted down the street and disappeared in the lunch crowd.

"Jack, Jack, Jack wait!" She yelled after him. She started to run through the crowd and then stopped. It was too late. He was gone. "Now what have I done?" She asked tears rolling down her face. She was standing on the sidewalk outside the church when Reverend Odamtey found her half an hour later.

When she got home that evening, she found Jack fast asleep on the sofa, looking disheveled, with shirt tails up above his stomach, smelling like a bar. She hurried to the refrigerator and grabbed a bottle of ice-cold water, opened it, took a long swallow and walked back to the sofa.

"Jack! Wake up! Where the hell have you been?" Serwah yelled, the pitch of her voice steadily climbing. "

How dare you walk away and leave me in the middle of the street like that? Wake up right now before I freeze your balls!"

"Mnnnn... "Jack turned over in his sleep. "Who are you... uh?" He mumbled sleepily.

"Your wife! Jack Ashong wake up right now!" Serwah swung the bottle of ice-cold water about two feet above Jack's bare mid-section. A drop of water slid off the bottom of the bottle and splashed on his nose. He sniffed loudly, licked his lips and opened one eye slowly.

"Ah Serwah," Jack said with a slurp,

"You look beeuuutiful. I am a lucky man." he added, belched and then continued, "When we get married..."

"We are married!" Serwah interjected. "You're drunk. You filthy, rotten-fish-smelling, cow-dung-filled-horse-shit, over-sized testicles, slimy, lecherous, irresponsible, confused sweetheart. Jack, how could you do this to me? And on our wedding day too? Why?"

He just stared at Serwah with glazed eyes, licking his lips. "I.. I... had ... did not know what... I ... Serwah, I sorry, very, sorry."

"Oh Jack, look at you." Serwah put down the ice water bottle and jumped on him. Somewhere between the moment she landed on him and the mixture of compassion and desire on her face, instant sobriety set in. Jack's hormones performed a miraculous changing of the guards. The couch groaned. Jack took her like a possessed man. That was how Tawiah was conceived.

Five-year-old Tawiah was trying to count from one to fifteen with her fingers. Every time she got to eleven, she would forget which finger she'd just counted and so she would start all over again. Lantey, who would soon be five, was watching her with an amused look on his face. He always found an excuse to wander over to Tawiah's to play whenever he got back from school. Home, his, was next door. Their parents knew each other well. Serwah and Lantey's mother, Adoley, were always borrowing each other's pots and pans. The joke between their husbands was, "Your fire, my pot, your food, my wife, it doesn't matter, as long as we are fed!" Then, they'll slap each other across the back and laugh heartily. This was their favorite skit, whenever Tawiah and Lantey played their grown-ups game. You could hear their high-pitched giggles as they chased each other across the yard.

Tawiah liked having Lantey around. It made her feel important. Kind of like the way her father made her

Mama feel special, calling her Mama lady, my queen and all those other big fat words. Daddy was always doing or saying something funny to her mother. Mama would say laughing, sometimes hysterically, "Why did I marry a crazy man like you?" Dad would wink and roar, "I tried to warn you. But no, you wanted me, bushman and all!" They'd laugh, shove each other playfully, then embrace and dance to the highlife music playing on the radio, singing on the top of their voices. Wow! Grown-ups were sooo much fun! She would get so excited at times that she would dash out the house to look for Lantey.

"Let's play grown-ups. You'll be the boy, I am the lady. Okay? Ready? No, wait. I'll be right back!" Tawiah would disappear into the house, and head straight for her mother's wardrobe. Five pairs of high heels, a dozen head-kerchiefs and three layers of rainbow-face make-up later, she would swish and sway out of the house, head held up high, like a princess heir of some northern village chief's serfdom. Lantey would giggle, pump his chest, and walking on his toes, come over and take Tawiah's hand. They would dance around the yard, laughing and screaming till dusk.

Lantey sighed, and said to himself, "Those were the

good old days." He was sitting at the curb at the roadway entrance to St. Aurora's Convent. He remembered their secondary school days. Students were not allowed to receive phone calls or make any calls for that matter. So when someone came to the dormitory to get you to take a phone call, everybody knew it had to be an emergency. Except Lantey. Tawiah found the most ingenious ways to get the head master, Mr. Reginald Baffoe, to put Lantey on the line. Lantey smiled and when he recalled the time she faked a nervous breakdown on the phone. Poor Mr. Baffoe, he dropped the heavy Bakelite telephone on his foot in his hurry to get him. Other times were not so funny, like when she called him crying on the phone.

He had just returned to school at Cape Coast after spending the summer holidays in Accra. They did not see much of each other that summer. He was sixteen and very restless. Tawiah was busy helping out at her mother's stall in the market. She liked Makola market. It was always bustling with activity, and an endless stream of new faces. That was where she first saw Mr. Samir Zahedi, one of many expat Lebanese businessmen living in the city. He introduced himself as an old friend of her mother, and vaguely commented on how much Tawiah had grown up just as beautiful as her mother. Right away she did not trust him and soon forgot about him. Three days later he was back. He did not come directly to their stall this time. He stood about twenty feet away, across from another stall and carefully watched Tawiah. After about an hour, he left without saying a word. She thought that was strange. So that evening when her mother came to help her close up the stall, she asked Serwah quietly, "Mom, who is this Sami Fahedi?" Serwah froze in her tracks.

"Zahedi? Samir came here? What did he want?" Serwah almost dropped the Dutch wax prints she was putting away.

"I don't know Mom. I thought you would. He said he was a friend of yours." Tawiah replied cautiously. "I would not have asked you except that this afternoon he came back and stood over there at Mrs. Agyeman's," Tawiah pointed to the stall across theirs, "and just stared at me," she added.

"Did Ruby speak to him? Why didn't she get rid of him?" Serwah asked quickly. Ruby Agyeman was a girlfriend of hers from their OAU balls days.

"Mom, what's the matter? Is he really a friend of yours? What should I do if he comes back here?" Tawiah asked concerned.

"Don't do anything! Don't speak to him and don't tell your father a word about this. Do you hear me?" Tawiah nodded. "I have to find that fool, Asiedu," Serwah whispered to herself then turned to her daughter. "You take the cab and go home as soon as Kwame gets here." Kwame was the cab driver on contract with them that summer to take Tawiah back and forth between their house in Mamprobi and the market.

Half an hour later, Serwah saw Tawiah off at the curb side and hurried to the corner to hail the next cab.

"Where to Ma'am?" The cab driver asked.

"Adabraka, and hurry!" Serwah replied

"Yes, Ma'am. We'll get you there in no time. I know all the shortcuts to avoid this bad traffic." The cabbie said with a smile.

Twenty minutes later they approached Adabraka. "Slow down. Let me see. The house should be three streets from the next traffic light. It's the first house on the corner. Faster!" Serwah yelled.

"You want to drive the car yourself Ma'am?" The cab driver glared at Serwah in his rear view mirror.

"I'm sorry. It's very important that I see this man quickly. My daughter may be in trouble." Serwah apologized.

"Abai!! Children!" The driver spat out. "These days they can be big trouble. I have three boys. Don't worry Ma'am, we'll get you there very soon. My cab, James Dean, is old but it can still move. One more curve, Ma'am. Ah, here we are." He added with a smile as he pulled James into the bougainvillea bushes in front of a pink house with bright green shutters.

Serwah grabbed her purse, gave the driver 1500 cedis and jumped out of the cab. "Ma'am, your change!" The driver yelled, but Serwah was already halfway along the side of the house, heading for the backdoor. The driver threw up his hands in the air, grabbed the steering wheel, quickly backed out the well-tended hedge and raced off before "This crazy woman returns to her senses," he thought aloud to himself.

Serwah prayed it was still there. She groped under the flower box outside the kitchen door in the back. The key was still there. Asiedu had always left the house key for her under the flower box when they used to go out to-gether. It was a two-story house with large rooms and long windows. Like most of the houses on the street, the windows had shutters on them to keep out the bright, hot sun. Two large bedrooms, one smaller bedroom and a huge bathroom were upstairs. The living room, kitchen, dining room, den and a small office were downstairs. The kitchen opened into a large dining area, which was used only on those special occasions when Asiedu had company he wanted to impress. Most of the time they ate in the kitchen. The hot meals were placed in large clay bowls and porcelain plates on a mat on the floor. They sat on low stools carved from odum tree trunks by master craftsmen in Asiedu's village. The village was about one hundred miles north of the city. She unlocked the door and walked through the kitchen, into the house. She was about to open her mouth and call out his name when she heard a noise. It seemed to be coming from upstairs. Then she heard a slow long moan followed by a sharp crack. She stopped and stood still. "Oh", she thought to herself, "That man is still kinky. Who is he with now?" Just as she was about to walk back into the kitchen, the door to the living room on her left opened, Asiedu walked out with a scotch and soda in his hand.

"Serwah! What a...?" Asiedu started almost dropping his drink.

"Who is that upstairs? Asiedu, you haven't changed one bit. What the hell is Samir Zahedi doing talking to my daughter?" Serwah asked, her voice rising. "You better tell your filthy friends to keep their dirty hands off my daughter! Do you hear me? I said Asiedu do you hear me? What is going on upstairs? No, I don't want to know!

"Keep your voice down, Serwah." Asiedu said gently. "I have a proposition for you. Samir is looking for some models, and I suggested Tawiah. You know he just opened a new textile factory near Akosombo. He just needs some nice young girls to model some of the new cloth designs. How many times has he been to your stall, twice? He told me he was very impressed with Tawiah. She has the right looks for what he wants. Samir is upstairs. Why don't you wait here, I'll get him and we can make a deal right now."

"Kojo Asiedu, don't you go nowhere. I do not like your Zahedi. I don't trust him. My daughter will have nothing to do with him or any of your schemes. Who do you think you are, strutting back into my life after all these years? I am a married woman with a family to take care of. Get off my face, I don't have time to waste here."

"Mister and Miss God! Who do you think you're fooling?" Asiedu asked, staring at Serwah with red, cold eyes. "You can't turn down my offer I know you have money troubles. That worthless drunk of a musician you call a husband has not been able to find any real work in months. The last band he played in broke up. He hasn't worked since that retired army General, Sakyi Prempeh, lost the presidential election last year. How are you going to pay Tawiah's school fees in September? How are you going to feed your expensive taste for jewelry, clothes and European shoes? Look," he opened a box on the floor near the door to the dining room, "Samir just received this shipment of shoes, bags and dresses from Rome. The latest fashion, aren't they beautiful? This red dress," he pulled out a low-cut lycra dress from the box, "will look very good on you." So think carefully before you open your mouth, my friend."

"Your friend? Your friend?? Do you know what that word means?" Serwah asked him, eyeball to eyeball. "You have no shame. Whose daughter is that upstairs with your friend, my friend?" She sneered at him. "Tell me, how much money did you make luring her to that filthy man up there? Did she model too? With or without clothes? Abai!!! Asiedu, do you think I'm stupid?" Serwah asked him, eyeballs still squared. She took a deep breath, stepped back, and shook her head slowly, looking him up and down then, with a hint of anger and pity she continued, "How very quickly we forget. Eh? I will never need your charity. It's tainted with all kinds of thievery and bribery, I'd rather not mention. So you keep your dung-smeared hands off my daughter and I'll keep my mouth shut!" Asiedu drink flew out of his hands as he lunged at her. But Serwah had anticipated this and quickly stepped out of the way. Asiedu's fist shot past her and rammed into the dining room wall. The Labadi Beach picture on the wall came crashing down as Serwah reached the back door of the house. She tried to kick off the high heel shoe on her right foot but it was too tight, so she grabbed her ankle to remove the other one. Asiedu reached her just as she pulled it off. He pounced on her with a raised bloody fist. Serwah swung around quickly on her bare left foot and kicked him in the groin as his bleeding fist slammed into the middle of her chest. Her left heel flew into the air as she fell back against the kitchen sink gasping for air. Asiedu grabbed his crotch screamed on top of his lungs.

"She wants to kill me! She's mad! She wants to kill me! She's mad! Help! Samir, come quickly!! Asiedu cried bent over in pain.

Serwah caught her breath and calmly picked up her left shoe and quickly pulled off the right heel. She turned to walk out the door then changed her mind. She walked back to Asiedu, pushed him against the sink and kicked him in the stomach then hit him on the head with both shoes screaming on top of her lungs, "Stay away from Tawiah! Stay away from my child, you hear me? You wretched limp noodle, irresponsible donkey's ass mockery of a man !" Asiedu let go of his crotch and lunged at her again, but Serwah was still too quick for him. She jumped out of his reach and slammed her knee between his legs from behind, propelling him into the swinging back door. As the door hit him in the head and bounced him back towards her. Serwah dropped both shoes and met his face with her fists. She slapped his face three times before Samir and his model Naa Ami pulled them apart.

Blood was oozing off Asiedu's head. Serwah's blouse was ripped and her bra was hanging off her left shoulder with blood from Asiedu's hand dripping off her chest.

"Call Dr. Ziad and tell him it's an emergency. I have to take Asiedu to see him immediately", Samir said to Naa Ami, "And get rid of her before I return", he added, pointing at Serwah. "Stay here till I get back, Naa Ami. Go put on some clothes!" He yelled at her as he pulled on his trousers grabbed Asiedu and dragged him out of the house.

Serwah leaned against the kitchen sink and burst out laughing loudly. Naa Ami dropped the phone, grabbed a newspaper and covered her chest. "Call me a taxi, you poor child. I'll let myself out." She said to Naa Ami, and burst out laughing again.

FOUR

ONE WAY TICKET TO KANO

Two more years, two more years and I will have that red sports car. I have watched Mr. Oshigbade drive that machine and wave at all the girls too many times with a rock in my belly. I have always had to struggle for everything I ever got in life; respect, promotion, lovers, secondary school certificate, university degree, suit, a good pair of black shoes, you name it. Why did my parents have to be so broke? Well, so they told me. The other boys on the block went to special boarding schools run by British expatriates. I went to the dirty public school across town with the outside latrines. People avoided that side of the street. The city girls took one look at you and laughed, "Oh, look at Eddie so-and-so, he goes to the shit school! Would you go out with him? No, no, never! He will ruin your perfume and reputation."

Life at the university was different though. It seemed the professors did not like any of us. The rigorous course work and endless reports kept us so busy. No one cared where you came from or went. My mother, however, still does not understand how an educated man like me prefers to work at the American-style carwash. Working for the government can be hazardous. That is where all my friends who did not go overseas for more book learning went to work. I learn more from the streets. Red sports car can evoke a more distinct reaction from around here than a piece of paper from a government office. Besides, I will not work for a government I cannot see. The head of the country is always in his camouflage suit.

"Now, how can you work for a man dressed like a tree?" I asked Peter Yakoto, during our regular evening fill up of cold beer at The Fulani Garden Terrace. Peter sported a Che Guevara beard with George Clinton dark glasses and a Harrison Ford hat to boot. Of course, how could I forget his authentic cowboy boots from Laredo, Texas. Peter was crazy about American music, movies, politics and even food, from that quickie hamburger meat place! I'm sorry my friend, I like to take my time to eat. First, I wash my hands slowly, with good home-made tar soap and lukewarm water. Next, test the temperature of the fresh palm nut soup with my middle finger, lick it good, then break off a bite-size piece of boiled yam, just off the fire, to stir the soup with, before honoring my tongue with the fruits of the sweat of the talented cook. Eating is a ritual I do not take lightly. Besides, the aroma, taste and the elegant spread of fresh cooked food is a priceless aphrodisiac. It always works, I know. That is how Marina caught me in her net. Granted, I helped her by inviting myself over for dinner. The woman knows how to cook, in the kitchen or anywhere else in the house for that matter!

Peter adjusted his hat and peered at me over his dark glasses. "You really should stop by and talk with Batata, he'll fix you up with that surveyor post I told you about. I already spoke to him about you. What do you think brother man?"

"Peter I don't know. I do not feel comfortable working in an office, especially a government office. What do you guys do with all those letters you write anyway? No don't tell me."

"Man, you need connections to survive in West Africa today. Get with the program. Look at you, man, you are an educated brother. You don't even own a jalopy. That's sad...", Peter looked across the terrace and whistled softly. "Ladies like her make you wish you drove a Rolls. It's unfortunate brother, you don't even own a Volkswagen."

"She is a looker all right." I said. "I recognize her. One of the Oshigbade trophies. Damn bastard!" I muttered under my breath.

"Oh yeah. Oshigbade's slamming. With that red rocket he zooms around him, he's hot. You're not. Man, what's with you and this morality shit? Lighten up and get laid. I guarantee you, every night."

"I don't know, Peter, with all these folks, some of whom I've always respected, dying of some dreadful disease. No thanks, No thanks Peter, I'll stick to Marina. I dig her and I know she's clean."

"There you go with that morality crap again. Ice it man." Peter retorted, then switched characters on me. "Jah noh! Trust in Jah, man. Do I look dead, man?"

"No, Mr. Cool, you may be soon if you don't slow down, my friend." I said to him gently. Peter winked and smiled, then looked across the room.

"Waiter!" He yelled. A young man in a starched white jacket hurried to our table. "Another round, make that a double. I think my friend here needs some libation and courage for what's coming." Peter said and winked at the lovely young lady we had been appreciating a few minutes ago. She winked back, swung out of her seat in helical slow motion, and jiggled provocatively towards our table. All the men in the place, with or without spouses, paramours or sweethearts, slobbered into their drinks.

"Hello, Peter, who is your friend?" She asked in a strong clear voice. "I'm Bissa," she added smiling at me.

"Joseph Ikwanemi. How do you do?" I replied with a smile.

"Fine, Joe... Joseph? Haven't I seen you somewhere before?" Bissa asked me.

"Joe is a computer programmer for Oshigbade's car wash." Peter answered before I could get a word in.

"Oh, you must be a brain! Computers! Clarence didn't tell me his carwash was so sophisticated! Mnnn, I guess that's why he didn't take me with him to America last year. That computer must have cost a fortune."

"I do not... " I started.

"Joe is also a great dancer." Peter butted in. "He and I won several dance competitions at the University. Hey man, do you still play those slick guitar solos?" He innocently asked with a wink.

"Goodness Joe, how come we haven't met yet? Musician, dancer, computer expert, and very good-looking too! You must be a very busy man." Bissa said perking up.

"Yes, Ms. Bissa, as a matter of fact I must be going. I have an appointment in fifteen minutes with a client."

"Someone gorgeous?" Bissa teased. "Come, Joe. I can stand a little competition. The girls in this town are wimps. Things have been rather boring here of late. Think I'll return to London next week for a quick visit." Then she added. "But who is she? Come on, Joe, you can tell me."

I smiled sheepishly. "Her name is Marina." Peter coughed, pulled his hat over his face and slowly shook his head.

"Marina, mmnnn, nice name too. When can I meet her? Maybe we can become good friends. I don't have any close girlfriends here. Just men, and you know what they all want. That's why I like Clarence. He always tells me he sees more in me than my gorgeous body. Joe, do I have a nice body? Honestly, tell me. Do you like it?" Bissa asked.

"Bissa, you have a very nice body."

"What are you talking about man? This sister's bod will kick the roof off a hundred-year-old man's hood!... Well, whatever's left of it. Do you need glasses? Get with the program, man. Shell out some expletives, and do justice to this divine beauty before your very eyes...", Peter was on a roll. "...or at least, do some vice or something", he added sotto voce. Bissa was beaming. She leaned over and gave Peter a peck on the cheek. I coughed.

"Peter, I really have to get going. Marina's fixed my favorite dish tonight." I said.

"Go on man, go." Peter sounded annoyed.

"She cooks too? Ai yaya! I hate girls who cook. My mother was too busy chasing some government man to teach me. Bitch." Now Bissa was getting upset.

"Bissa, I will never work for the government. You can count on that." I assured her.

"Joe, you are sweet, ... and probably broke too. But that's okay. I still like you. When can we go dancing?"

"Yeah, man, let's check out that new resort on the beach. I hear there's a hot band from Zaire there this weekend." Peter informed us.

"Can Marina dance too, Joe?" Bissa asked.

"Marina, ... damn I gotta go." I said glancing at my watch.

"Everybody does. Go ahead. Somewhere over there, not in my beer." Peter said and laughed.

"Shut up, Peter. You're disgusting!" Bissa said. She opened her pocketbook and turned to me. "Here's my number," she said and handed me a card. "Call me, maybe we can do some programming together." Bissa winked and added, "in my own high level language. L.O.V.E."

"Oooh man you better take that card quick, because if you don't I will." Peter said grinning.

"Thank you Bissa. It was a pleasure meeting you. I will call you very soon." I said and put her card in my wallet. Bissa leaned towards me.

"Don't wait too long, sweet Joe. Second chances are the only luxury items I don't care for." said Bissa. "Wait Joe, you never told me if Marina could dance?" She asked then added. "No, don't tell me. I don't know if I want to meet the..."

"You'll get along well with her, Bissa." I quickly interjected and as Peter told me later, kept running my big mouth, "she's wonderful, you'll really like her. Thanks for the lovely chat." I grabbed my jacket, swung it across the front of my trousers and left quickly.

"Is he always like that?" Bissa asked Peter before I made it across the terrace..

"Like what?" He asked.

"Oh, polite and... and, well..." Bissa giggled. "... rushing off with an erection." Peter groaned, then laughed.

"Well, my brother isn't alone. The temperature of half the fellas in this joint has already vaporized the mercury. That's the good news. You smoke 'em. The bad news Baby is that, you stoked him for Marina. She's getting a good work out tonight."

"Damn you! I'll make you pay for this. I'm cutting you off, and if you ever ring my doorbell again, I'll answer the door with my butcher's knife and... "Bissa paused and hissed, ".. I'll cut off that filthy..."

"Too bad Bissa." Peter interrupted her. "Joe's going places. Oshigbade trusts him completely. The State Office of Commerce just approved a license for him to open three new car washes. Joe will probably be running one of them. Clarence told the Minister this morning. Chill, Bissa. If you really dig the brother, I can pull a few strings. You and I,..."

"I don't ... "

"Wait, Bissa. I'm cool. You know, we always..." Peter started. Bissa smiled sweetly, picked up Peter's beer glass, poured the full glass of cold beer onto his lap and walked out the terrace, head up high, hips busy.

The phone and his hangover were out to get him. Peter shook his head and snatched the phone off the hook with clenched teeth.

"Don't you have any respect for...

"For God's sake, shut up Peter. Did you have a good time with Ms. Bissa Anna Funde last night?"

"Oh, it's Mr. Ikwanemi, the Holy Spirit himself." Peter groaned into the mouth piece. "Man, you almost blew that one. This is the last time I'm going to set you up."

"Peter, good friend, thanks for everything, but I happen to be already very much in love with a beautiful and sweet woman right here, who has something to say to you." Marina picked up the extension phone.

"Shit, wait Joe!"

"Hi, Peter, still hung over I see." Marina said with her usual cheery voice. "When are you coming over for dinner? My brother just brought over some sweet yams from his farm up north. I can cook some with my special green leaf stew for you and Joe tonight."

"Marina, dear, that bush rabbit skunk does not deserve you. I will make you my queen. Leave that pauper and marry me immediately." Peter said speaking in a proper Oxford accent. Joe laughed heartily.

"I will gladly trade places with you, just to see you domesticated. Felix the Cat gets married and settles down!" I said still laughing.

"By the way, Peter, we have some good news to share with you." Marina piped into the phone.

"Oh no, I'm going to be a godfather."

"No." Marina and I said in unison.

"I'm going to be a guardian angel."

"Lord help us, no." I said. "One more guess," Marina added.

"I'll fix you guys. I'll make you this one disgusting... Let me see, you're going to make me king and staff my palace with six harems, one for each..."

"Shut up, Peter." Marina said it this time. "Do you remember Joe's uncle who passed away last year?"

"Yeah, the one with all that cash money? How can I forget that?"

"Well, he left Joe his red 1988 BMW convertible, his house in Kano," said Marina, "and this is the part I don't like... his three youngest wives." she added quietly.

"When is dinner? Marina, did you say three youngest wives? See, I wasn't that far off. I have been seriously considering settling down of late. The least I can do is purchase our plane tickets to Kano." Peter said laughing from his belly.

"Don't worry about that, Peter dear." Marina said happily, "Joe already bought you a one-way plane ticket to Kano."

FIVE

GULF OF GUINEA

A fleet of European ships arrived in Elmina at dawn sometime in 1536. Our great-great-great-second-uncle-twice-removed, Ansah, was not very popular with the villagers. He was accused of selling his own to the white man. Ansah's taciturn response was that, he was only trying to make a living. After failing to seduce his cousin's wife, Awura Boatema-Serwa, sometimes called Awurama by the locals, he concocted some story and squealed on him to Captain Joaquim Da Gama's right-hand man. Before Awura Boatema-Serwa could tell her beloved what really happened, he was captured and never seen again. According to the custom then, the wife of a "dead" man was required to live with a male next-of-kin of the deceased. Awurama bit her tongue and moved her things into Ansah's household.

Their first night together, which he never forgot for the rest of his life, was one Ansah should have cherished, but then what happened to him was akin to a long-tongued hungry frog snatching the last morsel of mango meat from you just when you are ready to eat it. Ansah disrobed and right in the middle of rubbing his hands and smiling with glee, Boatema-Serwa glared back at him, and with a sharp hiss pushed him down, mounted him swiftly without taking her eyes off his awe-stricken face, and then ravished him over and over and over again till daybreak, ignoring his cries for clemency, mercy, pardon in six different languages! None of the lower Sahara medicine men, witch doctors and bushmen healers from Ouagadougou to Afadjato, or Songhai to Tanganyika could exorcise the angry spirit that took residence in his lower back. Thus, Ansah, once the proud predator of nubile young women, was reduced to the posture of a castrated praying mantis.

Awura Boatema-Serwa gave birth to a fine healthy son, after the second rains and harvest. She nurtured him properly, taught him to respect himself and his elders. Most important of all, she warned him to keep the weapon between his legs under control, especially in the presence of nubile young women. When he was old enough to understand the story, one of his not so discrete friends in the village told him how his father obtained his famous posture. Kojoaben was shocked, but his respect for his mother went up another notch. He listened to Awura Boatema-Serwa carefully and gave his mother very few problems. Well, until soon after he turned fifteen.

By the age of fourteen Kojoaben had become quite an accomplished fisherman. He liked the ocean. So, when he was eight, his mother did not stop him from spending a lot of time with his uncle, Sackey, a fisherman. Ocean fishing with a small fishing net from a canoe was not easy. Uncle Sackey was a good teacher. His nephew learned fast and the earnings he brought in from the fishing helped the household. This was the other reason why his mother did not complain.

Uncle Sackey was from another tribe and had left his clan when he married an Elmina woman. Elmina women were well known far and wide for their beauty and gentle, sweet temperament. Boatema-Serwa, Kojoaben's mother, was not from Elmina. She was an Ashanti, proud and defiant, the daughter of a prince. When she was fifteen, she was abducted by rebels during an ambush of the prince's entourage, en route to a neighboring serf kingdom. Boatema-Serwa did not care for Elmina women. The feeling was mutual, thus the prefix "Awura" (or Lady!), before her first name Boatema. She thought them weak, foreign and wishy-washy. When he was younger, Kojoaben who was of course, born and raised in Elmina, played with both the little girls and boys in the neighborhood whenever his mother let him. He was not drawn to any one in particular, until the last annual fish fry, which took place just after his fifteenth birthday.

The fish fry was held on the beach all week long under the full moon in August. Kojoaben and his uncle Sackey had just returned from an early evening fishing trip. They had a good trip. The singing and dancing was just beginning as their boat, full of fresh fish glistening in the silver moonlight, pulled into the bay. A number of their colleagues rushed to meet them as they jumped out of the canoe and helped them push the full canoe ashore. Already, a large crowd of people had started gathering around the dancers and drummers. Kojoaben could not wait to take the best of the catch to his mother so he could hurry back to the beach. For an Ashanti woman, Boatema-Serwa had quickly learned to enjoy cooked fresh fish. A delicacy for the Ashantis, which even the prince, her father, rarely enjoyed in their inland empire. She could never understand how such wishy-washy wo-menfolk like these Elmina women could fix fish in so many tantalizing ways. Bah! If she could go back to her father's house, she would admonish her maids, servants and teachers for not teaching her such important cooking arts. No wonder Elmina women were so much in de-mand! "I know things that they would never know!" She would say to herself and add, "They are all ignorant, lazy servants and weak Elmina women!"

Kojoaben never made it home with the fresh fish that night. This was the first reason why Boatema-Serwa's heartbreak was twice as painful. Arafua, the young wom-an who really meant no harm, was the attraction which led to Kojoaben's distraction, the cause for Boatema-Serwa's second heartbreak. Arafua was nineteen and the acknowledged village beauty. Somehow, she eluded the advances of Captain Joaquim Da Gama and his first of-ficer. The Portuguese did not like this. They felt entitled to anything and everything in Elmina. After all, they got here first. Not the ridiculous Spaniards, not the dizzy British, not the crazy Dutch, and certainly not these stupid Negroes in this hot accursed place!

Arafua had often seen Kojoaben when she went to the open outdoor fish market to shop for her mothers. The market was located close to the bay. Kojoaben always greeted her politely. She thought he was a nice boy but she never looked at him twice. Her father's wives sent her to market because she got the best fish at ridiculous prices. Her family ate well. When Kojoaben turned fourteen Arafua started to pay a little more attention whenever they met in the market. "He is cute", she would say to herself, "but he is only a boy. He hasn't fathered a son yet." That night of the fish fry something changed her assessment of him.

Kojoaben had been so excited about the festivities that he took the wrong turn on the way home. Soon he found himself lost in the thick brush growing beneath the cliffs overlooking the bay. He decided to retrace his steps back to the beach to find the right path. He was almost back to the old path when a slight movement between some rocks on the shore caught his eye. There, bathing in the moonlight, stood the most beautiful woman he had ever seen. At first all he saw was her back. She must have been about fifteen feet from where he stood in the middle of the brush about two feet high, under a cluster of coconut trees. He quickly looked around to see if anyone had seen him. Then he remembered that he had overheard some of the fishermen talking about a secluded spot where the women of Elmina sometimes went alone to bathe in the ocean. Kojoaben had never seen a woman bathing before. Certainly never one wearing nothing but a few rows of tiny sparkling beads. She slowly scooped the cool ocean water with her hands and lovingly poured it over her full breasts and shapely body. He watched with his heart in his throat. "God in Heaven help me! She is beautiful!" He whispered aloud to himself and dropped his bag of fresh fish. She must have heard something because she suddenly turned around and saw him.

"Kojoaben!" she exclaimed

"Arafua! I am sorry. I did not mean to be snooping. I .... I ... got lost. I   was on my way ho...ho... home, to...to... to give ...my my Mama some ..fi fi..fre...fresh fish." Kojoaben stammered, eyes lowered, staring in the brush.

"Come here." Arafua said quietly over the soft lapping of the waves against the rocks. Kojoaben took two steps back and bumped into a coconut tree. He got up and stumbled again, falling face forward into the end of the brush.

"I promise, I will never tell anyone I saw you." He said unhappily, and then pleaded with her, "Please Arafua, okay?"

"Don't worry, by the time I'm done with you, you won't be able to speak for quite a while." Arafua answered, stepped out of the water and started walking slowly towards him with a mischievous soft smile on her face. "Get up and look at me." She added. Kojoaben crawled up and sat in the sand holding his head in his hands. He started shivering. Arafua knelt down beside him, pulled his hands away from his head and kissed him. She pushed him back gently into the sand and took him, three times for starters. This boy was not like the others. She liked him even more because he did not know what he was doing to her, and the icing on the cake was, he did not know what he had. At first he was so embarrassed that he tried to hide it. Until it split his loin cloth and burst out of his torso crackling like a hot large yam roasting on charcoal fire! Oh what a night for courting satisfaction! So many times, it happened so many times she lost track of everything. The waves of rapture crashing within her and the ocean waves crashing against the rocks became one. She would start cresting and rise up twenty feet high, a huge wave rushing towards the shore to crash against the rocks in ecstasy. She was at the junction, the place her mothers' mothers and the medicine women of the tribe spoke about. The place where fire and water met, where she could only gasp for air, if air was not too busy keeping fire and water apart. That fire and water was all he saw in her eyes when she opened them long enough to look at the moon. She felt possessed, unable to stop. Then she looked into his eyes and cried out loud. "Save me!" and crashed again, collapsing on top of him.

They lay still as the tide rose. The waves gently washed their young exhausted bodies. Kojoaben woke up first just as the first light of dawn peeped over the horizon. He took her hand and pulled her up to higher ground. He helped her find her clothes and together they just about floated into the village just before sunrise.

The next morning, her mothers congratulated her on the delicious fish she brought home that day before. They were all excited because word had started spreading in the village that their household had won the fish fry competition.

Awura Boatema-Serwa took her frustration out on Ansah, her son's father. That night, the second time in her life she took him, two angry spirits pulled his back apart till it broke. Right after the funeral, Kojoaben left the village in a canoe with Arafua, never to return to Elmina again.

SIX

NOTES

A little background information on the short stories in this book:

1) Gulf of Guinea:

A number of West African countries along the coast of the Gulf of Guinea are the setting for the stories in this book. Located along the west coast of Africa, running from Cape Three Points in Western region of Ghana (4.744°N 2.089°W) to Cape Lopez in Gabon (0°38'S 8°42'E), two major rivers the Volta and the Niger drain in to the Gulf to merge with the Atlantic Ocean.

2) Ga-Mashie:

A historically significant area where the Ga people originally settled. Ga-Mashie, which includes the communities of Ussher Town and James Town, is also known as Old Accra and is located along the southwest coast of Accra, the capital of Ghana.

3) Homowo:

This is a harvest festival historically celebrated to mark the end of a great famine suffered by the Ga and Ga-Adangbe people of Ghana. Homowo literally means "hooting at hunger". It is still celebrated annually with ceremonies, drumming, singing, dancing and special foods. The festival is a huge favorite for both locals and tourists.

4) Highlife (music):

Highlife is a music genre that started in Ghana. The style employed the melodies and rhythms / percussion of traditional Ghanaian music fused with western horns and catchy guitar riffs derived from jazz-influenced chord progressions. Highlife spread all over West Africa, especially in Nigeria where a number of popular sub-genres of the style evolved along with the addition of electric piano / organ, other native instruments and more sophisticated arrangements by highlife bands there, in Ghana, and other parts of Africa and Europe.

UNILAG: University of Lagos, located in Lagos, Nigeria

OAU: The Organization of African Unity, predecessor of the African Union (AU)

5) Labadi Beach:

This is one of the most popular and busiest beaches along the coast of Ghana. Dubbed La Pleasure Beach, located about 9 Km from Accra, the capital, Labadi Beach is also near Teshie in the Greater Accra region.

6) Kano:

Kano is the capital of Kano State in northern Nigeria. With a population of more than 2.5 million, it is the second largest city in Nigeria. Hausa is the main language spoken in Kano, which is home to many members of the Hausa tribe.

7) Elmina:

Elmina is a historically significant Ghanaian town located on the south coast of South Ghana in the Central Region. It sits on a south-facing bay on the Atlantic Ocean coast of Ghana; about 12 km west of the city of Cape Coast. Elmina, the first European settlement in West Africa, discovered by the Portuguese, was a major shipping port for moving slaves across the Atlantic during the heyday of the European slave trade. Slaves were kept in the dungeons of Elmina Castle until it was time to ship them to buyers in the Americas, Caribbean and Europe. It was the West African headquarters for Portugal's trade and exploitation of African resources. Originally the Portuguese's interest was gold but later expanded to include the sale of thousands of slaves shipped from Elmina.

8) The Ashanti / Ashantis:

The Ashanti region, home of the Ashanti people, is centrally located in the middle of Ghana. This is the most populated region of Ghana and it is known for gold and cocoa production. Kumasi, the capital of the region, is also home to the Kwame Nkrumah University of Science and Technology. Prior to the beginning of colonialism of Africa in the 15th century by the Europeans, the Kingdom of Ashanti which was already established and thriving, was one of the most stable and influential states in sub-Saharan Africa. The Ashantis were a powerful tribe undefeated by the British colonists.

ABOUT THE AUTHOR

Mr. Ashie originally from Ghana, is an engineer, musician, songwriter, arranger and producer. He completed his primary and secondary school education in Ghana before leaving for the United States to continue his education at an engineering college on the east coast. Throughout the years, he never gave up on his love of music. Starting in Accra, next to the shores of the Gulf of Guinea, he created studio recordings of popular West African music and originals. He also performed live with various bands in the city. This musical journey still thrives today here in the US with performances and production work for various groups and solo artists in the US, and other countries in Asia and Africa.

Gulf of Guinea

67

9 780996 997607